Jenika Sings for Freedom

Freedom

{ Jenika Chante pou Libète }

A Story in English and Kreyòl by the
Restavek Freedom Writers

Illustrated by Emily Iddings

Restavek Freedom Foundation

Shout Mouse Press

Restavek Freedom Foundation / Shout Mouse Press
Published by
Shout Mouse Press, Inc.
www.shoutmousepress.org

Copyright © 2014 Shout Mouse Press, Inc.

Authored by the Restavek Freedom Writers.
Transcribed in Kreyòl and English by Colleen Zamor and Laeticia Hollant.
Edited in English by Kathy Crutcher.
Translated in Kreyòl by Michelle Marrion.
Edited in Kreyòl by Christina Guérin.

Photography by Steven Baboun and Michelle Marrion.
Illustrated by Emily Iddings.

ISBN-13: 978-0692321515 (Shout Mouse Press, Inc.)
ISBN-10: 0692321519

To all kids who are going through hard times:
Know that one day your lives will shine.

To the adults who read this book:
Think about the children in your home and love them,
because the children are the future.

Pou tout timoun kap pase mizè oswa yon moman difisil:
Konnen yon jou lavi n' ap pi bèl.

Pou tout granmoun k'ap li liv sa a:
Panse ak timoun ki rete lakay nou.
Renmen yo, paske timoun se demen nou.

In the middle of the Caribbean lies a small island country where the sun is strong, the beaches are beautiful, and the trees are big with bright flowers.

HAITI.

Nan mitan Karayib la, gen yon ti peyi ki gen bon solèy, bèl plaj, ak gwo pye bwa k' gen bèl flè sou yo.

Peyi sa a rele AYITI.

Every morning when the sun comes up, the nightingales start to sing.

They fly over the green mountains, past the tap-taps on the street, and beyond the sugarcane fields, until eventually, one of them reaches a town on the sea and rests on Jenika's window.

The bird chirps its song and Jenika opens her eyes. When she sees the bird, she sings along with it her morning song:

Every morning I wake up,
I see the sun shining,
I put my two knees on the
floor and I start praying...
That's life...

Every morning
I wake up...

Chak maten
lè m' leve...

Chak maten lè solèy la leve, wosinyòl yo kòmanse chante. Yo vole sou tèt mòn vèt yo, yo pase anlè tap-tap yo sou lari a, yo vole sou chan kann yo, jiskaske youn nan yo rive nan yon ti katye bò lanmè sou fenèt kay Jenika.

Pandan wosinyòl la ap chante Jenika louvri je li, e li kòmanse chante ansanm ak ti zwazo a:

Chak maten lè m'leve , mwen wè solèy la klere,
mwen mete jenou m'atè epi m'kòmanse priye... Se lavi...

As she sings, Jenika's five brothers and four sisters wake up, too, and they also begin to sing.

As all the children sing, Jenika's parents wake up, too, and then everyone is up, and they begin the work of the day.

Jenika's mother prepares breakfast for everyone – coffee and bread -- but the food there isn't enough, so their coffee is thin, and their bread is small.

Lè Jenika kòmanse chante, tou lè senk frè ansanm ak kat sè li yo leve pou yo chante avèk li.

Manman ak papa Jenika tande tout timoun yo kap chante, yo tou leve e tout moun kòmanse mete aktivite nan kay la.

Manman Jenika pare manje pou tout moun – kafe ak pen – men, manje ki gen nan kay la pa sifi pou yo tout. Kafe a klè e moso pen yo piti.

While they eat, Jenika and her siblings watch the other children walk to school in their uniforms.

Jenika thinks, *I want to go, too!*

But Jenika and her siblings cannot go to school, for it is expensive and they have no money to spare. They have to stay home and help their mother with chores and prepare the house.

While they work, they sing.

Pandan yap manje, Jenika ak tout frè ak sè l'yo gade lòt timoun nan katye a kap mache ak inifòm yo sou yo, pou y' ale lekol. Nan tèt li Jenika konn panse, *Mwen ta renmen ale lekòl, tou!*

Men, Jenika ak lòt timoun nan kay la paka al lekòl, paske lekòl la twò chè. Yo oblije rete lakay pou ede manman yo fè menaj ak fè lòt travay nan kay la.

Pandan yap travay, yo toujou ap chante.

One afternoon, Aunt Sylvie arrives from Port-au-Prince to spend a week with the family. She is tired from the long trip.

She looks around the small crowded house and sees the poor conditions.
"Don't you have anywhere for me to lie down?" she asks.
She opens the pantry. "Where is all your food?"
She looks at all the children looking back at her. "And why don't the kids go to school?"

The family is embarrassed that Aunt Sylvie thinks their situation is so bad, and she quickly changes the subject.

Yon jou aprèmidi, Matant Silvi, rive sot' Pòtoprens pou l pase yon semèn avèk fanmi a.

Vwayaj la fatige l'.

Li gade toupatou nan ti kay la. Li wè nan ki move kondisyon yap viv.
Li mande: "Kibò mwen ka fè yon ti repoze la a?"
Li ouvè gadmanje a. "Kote manje a?"
Li gade tout timoun yo ki kanpe, y' ap gade' l tou. "Epi poukisa timoun yo pa ale lekòl?"

Fanmi an wont poutèt Matant Silvi ap panse yap viv mal anpil, men Matant Silvi vin chanje sijè a rapid.

By the end of the week when Aunt Sylvie is getting ready to go back to Port-au-Prince, she tells Jenika's mother, "*Cherie*, let me take Jenika with me. She can go to school, and I will take care of her and provide her with everything she needs."

Jenika's mother knows that she does not have the means to take care of all her children. She thinks Jenika will have a better life with her aunt. She does not want her to go, but she wants what is best for her daughter. "Ok," she says.

She is full of both sadness and hope.

Lè semèn lan fini, pandan Matant Silvi ap pare pou l' tounen Pòtoprens, li di manman Jenika, "Cheri, kite m' al lakay mwen ak Jenika. M' ap voye l' lekòl, m' ap pran swen l', e m'ap bali tout sa l' bezwen."

Manman Jenika pa vle kite l' ale, men, kòm li konnen li pa gen mwayen pou l' okipe tout timoun li yo, li panse Jenika kapab jwenn yon lavi miyò ak matant la. Li di, "Dakò."

Men li santi kè li lou an menm tan li gen espwa tou.

Jenika is sad to leave her family, but she is happy, too.

She can go to school! She can see the city! She has big hopes for her future and is ready for adventure.

She hugs each one of her siblings and gives her mother and father a kiss.

She waves goodbye from the back of the *tap-tap* going down the bumpy road.

An menm tan Jenika tris paske l' ap kite fanmi l', li gen kè kontan tou.

Li konnen l' pwale lekòl! Li konnen l' ap kapab wè kapital la! Li gen gwo espwa pou demen e li pare pou nouvo lavi sa a kap tann li.

Li anbwase fwè ak sè l' yo e li bay manman l' ak papa l' chak yon bo.

Li voye men ba yo pou di yo orevwa pandan li déyè tap-tap kap mennen l' ale a.

When Jenika arrives in Port-au-Prince, her aunt takes good care of her. She combs her hair, gives her nice clothes, and shows her affection. She tells her she is like her daughter. She gives her a nice room with a closet with pretty clothes inside. Jenika feels like it's a dream come true.

But soon, after a few weeks, everything changes.

⌐✄⌐

Lè Jenika fèk rive Potòprens, matant li byen okipe l'. Li penyen cheve l', bali bèl rad pou l' mete, epi li trè janti avèk li. Matant la di Jenika li se tankou pitit fi pa l'. Li bali yon bèl chanm nan kay la ak tout yon pandri chaje avèk bèl rad. Jenika santi tankou li nan yon bèl rèv.

Men, apre de twa semèn, bagay yo vin chanje.

On the morning of the first day of school when her cousins are getting ready, Jenika runs to her aunt and asks, "Will I go to school today, too, Aunt Sylvie?" Her aunt shoots her a cold look and says, "That is not why I brought you here."

Jenika is confused. "I don't understand, Aunt Sylvie. I thought you said you would send me to school with the other kids." But her aunt slapped her. "I didn't bring you here for school," she said. "I brought you here for work."

Lè premye jou lekòl la rive, Jenika wè kouzen l' yo nan maten kap pare pou yo soti. Lè l' wè sa, li kouri al jwenn matant li pou l' mande l', "Èske m' pwal lekòl jodi a tou, Matant Silvi?" Matant li ba l' yon kout je, epi l' reponn li: "Se pa pou sa mwen mennen w' isit la."

Jenika sezi poutèt li te konnen li ta pwal lekòl ansanm avek kouzen l' yo. "Mwen pa konprann, Matant Silvi, mwen te kwè ou te di ou ta pwal voye m' lekòl ansanm avèk lòt timoun yo?" Lè matant li tande sa, li ba Jenika yon kalòt epi li di: "Mwen pat mennen w' isit la pou lekòl, mwen mennen w' isit la pou travay."

Jenika runs outside to cry. As she cries, one of her cousins, Mark, who is much older and who has always been nice to her, comes to console her.

"Don't cry, Jenika," he says. "I will look out for you."

Her aunt looks out the window and says, "Jenika, I didn't bring you here to talk to Mark! Come inside to do your work."

Jenika enters with her head down and her heart beating in her belly. "The dishes are dirty," says her aunt. "And the floors need mopping. Hurry up!"

Jenika is an obedient child, so she begins to clean. As she soaps the dishes and scrubs the floors, she thinks of her family and her home by the sea. Her eyes get wet. She remembers a song her mother taught her and starts to hum it to give her strength.

Jenika kouri deyò a pou l' kriye. Pandan lap kriye, youn nan kouzen l' yo ki rele Mak vin konsole l'. "Pa kriye, Jenika. Pa dekouraje paske map toujou voye je sou ou."

Matant la parèt nan fenèt lan, e li di: "Jenika, mwen pa mete w' isit la pou vin bat bouch ou ansanm avèk Mak! Antre vin fè travay yo paske se pou sa mwen mete w' la a."

Jenika antre nan kay la ak tèt li bese avèk kè l' prèt pou vole nan lestomak li, tèlman lap bat fò. Matant li di konsa, "Veso yo sal, al lave yo! Epi pase mòp nan tout chanm yo. Fè rapid!"

Jenika, se yon timoun obeyisan. Li kòmanse pwòpte kay la. Pandan lap pase kim savon nan asyèt yo e pandan lap foubi seramik yo, li komanse panse ak fanmi l' e ak kay li bò lanmè a. Li tou sonje yon chante manman l' te aprann li e li kòmanse fredone ti chante a pandan lap travay pou li ka pran fòs.

Days pass, and then weeks, and then months, and then years. Jenika's life remains the same.

She cleans and she cries and she suffers. But she continues to sing, too, because this is the only thing that keeps her going.

Aunt Sylvie always discourages her when she hears her singing. "You will never be anything!" she says. "Stop making noise in my head with your rusty voice. Don't waste your time singing because you are no good."

Jenika gets discouraged, and she is so tired of her aunt's cruelty. She begins to believe maybe she is right. Maybe she will never be worth anything after all?

Gen anpil jou, semèn, avèk ane ki pase. Lavi Jenika rete menm jan an.

Li netwaye, li kriye, li soufri. Men, li pa janm sispann chante paske se nan sa li jwenn fòs li.

Matant Silvi toujou ap dekouraje l' lè lap chante. Li konn di l': "Ou pap janm anyen! Sispann fè bwi nan tèt mwen ak vwa feray ou a. Pa pèdi tan ou chante, ou pa menm gen bèl vwa."

Jenika santi l' dekouraje, li santi l' about ak jan matant la trete l'. Li kòmanse kwè nan sa matant la ap di li. Petèt li pap janm vin yon moun nan lavi a tout bon vre?

One day when Jenika can take it no more she goes outside in the yard, sits under a small lemon tree, and starts to talk to God.

"Am I not like everyone else? Do you want me to spend all of my life suffering like this?"

She is so sad and empty she can do nothing but cry. She asks God to please, please God, send someone to rescue her. Then she sings a song of hard times.

If you see that I'm crying,
there's a problem that I have...

Yon jou, Jenika soti deyò sou lakou a, anba yon ti pye sitwon e li kòmanse pale ansanm ak Bondye.

"Èske mwen pa menm jan ak tout moun?
Èske ou vle m' pase tout lavi m' ap pase mizè konsa?"

Li si tèlman tris li santi tèt li vin vid. Sèl bagay li ka fè se kriye. Li sipliye Bondye pou l' voye yon moun sou wout li pou retire l' nan sitiyasyon sa a. Epi, li chante yon chante kap rakonte youn nan moman difisil li yo.

Si ou wè ke map kriye gen yon pwoblèm mwen gen...

Mark, who has just come home from work, enters the yard and hears Jenika crying and singing. He stops to hear what she is saying, and it goes straight to his heart. Her voice is so beautiful, like the voice of an angel.

Mark sits down next to Jenika and says,
"You have value in my eyes,
and you have even more value in God's eyes.
One day, you will get out of this situation."

As Jenika cries on his shoulder, Mark understands that it is his obligation to save her.

Mak, te fèk sot travay, epi li pase nan jaden an. Pandan l' ap pase li tande yon bwi e li wè se Jenika kap kriye pandan l' ap chante. Mak kanpe pou l' tande sa chante a di, e mo li tande kap soti nan bouch Jenika yo, fwape l' tou dwat nan kè l'. Vwa a tèlman bèl, li sonnen tankou vwa yon zanj.

Mak chita bò kote Jenika e li di l',
"Ou gen anpil valè nan zye m' e nan zye Bondye ou gen plis valè.
Yon jou kanmèm wap soti nan sitiyasyon sa a."

Pandan Jenika ap kriye sou zepòl li, Mak wè se yon obligasyon li genyen pou l' sove li.

In the next weeks, Mark organizes a plan for Jenika's new home. He arranges to pay for her to live with a friend of his, so she does not need to work. Instead, she will go to school and to singing lessons. Mark makes Jenika promise that she will continue to sing despite Aunt Sylvie's discouragement.

"You have a gift," he says.

One day, while Aunt Sylvie is at work, Mark uses the opportunity to move Jenika out of the house. She is free!

Nan pwochen semèn yo, Mak fè yon plan pou Jenika. Li jwenn yon lòt fwaye pou li. Li peye pou Jenika al viv kay youn nan zanmi l' yo, yon kote li pa pwal travay. Nan plas travay la, Jenika pwale lekòl, epi lap pran kou chante tou. Mak fè Jenika pwomèt li pwal kontinye chante malgre tout dekourajman Matant Silvi te bay li.

Li di Jenika: "Ou gen yon don."

Yon jou pandan Matant Silvi al travay, Mak tou profite mennen Jenika ale. Jenika libere!

At first when Aunt Sylvie can't find Jenika, she looks for her. But when she doesn't find her, she says it's not important anyway.

"Jenika has no value, so it doesn't matter that she has left. I can just find another child to take her place."

Lè Matant la wè li pa janm wè Jenika ankò, li kòmanse chache l' toupatou. Lè li wè l' pa ka jwenn li, li di sa pa fè anyen.

"Jenika pa gen okenn valè, sa pa fè anyen si l' sove. Mwen annik jwenn yon lòt timoun pou pran plas li."

Many years pass, and Jenika works hard to prove her aunt wrong.

She studies and she practices.
She finds people who believe in her, and she believes again in herself.
And most importantly, she sings.

So when Mark hears about a national contest in Port-au-Prince to find the best singers in the country, he signs her up. He knows she has a beautiful voice, and he hopes that she can win.

Anpil ane pase, e Jenika travay di pou li pwouve matant li pat gen rezon.

Li etidye, epi li pratike chante a.
Li jwenn moun ki kwè nan li, epi li vin kwè nan tèt li tou.
E sa ki pi enpòtan, li pa janm sispann chante.

Lè Mak tande gen yon konkou nasyonal kap fèt nan Pòtorens pou yo jwenn tout pi bon chantè nan peyi a, li enskri Jenika ladan l'. Li konnen Jenika gen yon bèl vwa e li swete pou li ta genyen.

One day, Aunt Sylvie is flipping through the channels on TV and lands on a beautiful singing girl. She says, "Oh, listen to that voice! I must follow this show."

She watches until the end, when the judge hands the host an envelope that contains the name of the champion.

"And the winner is..." says the host. He pauses dramatically.

Yon jou, pandan matant Silvi tap chanje chenn nan televizyon, li tombe sou yon bèl tifi kap chante. Li di "O, gade jan yon tifi gen yon bèl vwa. Banm swiv sa lap fè a!"

Pandan lap swiv emisyon an, jij la bay animatè a yon anvlòp ki genyen non chanpyon konkou a landan'l.

Animatè a anonse, "Epi chanpyon an se ..." Li pran yon poz.

Aunt Sylvie peers closer at the screen. The same beautiful singing girl steps forward.
"No," Aunt Sylvie says.

But then her own son, Mark, appears on stage with this girl to take a picture. Together they smile and hold up the prize.

And then Aunt Sylvie knows it is really her. Jenika. She is stunned.

Matant Silvi kale je l' pi pre ekran an. Menm bèl ti fi ki tap chante a, avanse devan sèn nan.
Li di, "Non, se pa vre!"

Men lè sa a, li wè pwòp pitit gason li, Mak, parèt sou sèn la ak ti fi a pou fè yon foto. Yo souri ansanm e yo leve koup la anlè.

Se lè sa a Matant Silvi wè kiyès ti fi a ye. Se Jenika pa l' la.
Li sezi.

A few days pass.

Aunt Sylvie feels worse and worse about all the bad things she did to Jenika. Finally she cannot take the guilt anymore and calls Mark.

"Mark," she says. "I would like to meet with Jenika. I saw her on TV." Her voice breaks. "I was so terrible to her. Do you think she will see me?"

Kèk jou pase.

Kè Matant Silvi vin santi l' pi mal de jou an jou pou mizè. Li konnen l' te fè Jenika pase. Li sitèlman santi l' koupab, li rele Mak nan telefòn.

Li di: "Mak, mwen ta renmen rankontre ak Jenika. Mwen te wè l' sou televizyon." Epi pandan vwa l' kase, li di. "Mwen te fè l' twòp mechanste. Èske ou panse li tap dakò poul wè m'?"

The next day, Mark and Jenika go to meet Aunt Sylvie at her house. Jenika is nervous, but she feels strong. She is not the same little girl who once scrubbed these floors.

Aunt Sylvie looks the same, but older. She looks frail. She asks Jenika for forgiveness for all the bad things she did to her for all those years.

Jenika listens to all that Aunt Sylvie has to say.

Nan demen, Mak avèk Jenika al rankontre matant lan lakay li. Jenika yon jan pè, men li santi li gen plis fòs. Li pa santi l' se menm ti fi sa a ki te konn foubi seramik yo.

Figi Matant Silvi rete menm jan, men ou ka wè li vin pi granmoun. Li sanble l' fèb. Li mande Jenika padon pou tout move bagay li te fè l' pandan tout ane sa a yo.

Jenika tande tout sa matant li gen pou di l'.

Jenika sits quietly. There are so many things she does not understand.
How could her aunt have been so cruel?
Why did she feel she had the right to make someone feel worthless?
There are no excuses for the ways Aunt Sylvie treated her as a child.

But more than anything, Jenika wants to feel free. To let go of that pain and hear her aunt ask for forgiveness. That is freedom.

Jenika chita tou dousman. Gen anpil bagay li pa konprann.
Ki jan matant li te fè pou l' mechan konsa?
Sak fè l' te santi l' te gen dwa fè yon moun santi l' pa vo anyen konsa?
Li wè pa gen okenn eskiz pou fason Matant Silvi te trete l' lè li te timoun.

Men, plis pase tout bagay, Jenika vle santi li libere. Tande matant li kap mande l' padon fè l' lage doulè sa a li tap kenbe nan kè li. Sa se libète.

And so Jenika says,

"I forgive you,"

and it is done.

Se konsa, Jenika di:

"Mwen padonen w'."

Epi sa fini la.

When she gets home, Jenika thanks God as well as Mark.

"Thank you, Mark, for all you have done for me. It is thanks to you that I have gotten where I am today and that my life is now as beautiful as it is."

Mark says,

"You are the reason your life is beautiful, Jenika."

Lè li rive lakay li, Jenika remesye Bondye e li remesye Mak tou.

"Mèsi Mak pou tout sa ou fè pou mwen. Se gras a ou si mwen rive kote mwen ye jodiya, se gras a ou si lavi mwen ka bèl konsa kounye an."

Mak di,

"Se ou menm ki fè lavi w' bèl, Jenika."

Jenika smiles and she cries.

She feels so much happiness and so much gratitude that she does what she does best.

She sings.

⚬~≍~⚬

Jenika souri epi li kriye.

Li tèlman santi l' kontan e li tèlman rekonesan, li tonbe fè sa l' konn fè pi byen an.

Li chante.

The Story **BEHIND** The Story

Jenika is not a real little girl, but her story–of leaving her family, working as a servant, longing to go to school, and being denied the love and care she needs–is all too real for too many children in modern-day Haiti. These children are known as *restavek*.

What is *Restavek*?

Restavek is a Creole term that means "to stay with." Typically born into poor rural families, *restavek* children are sent to stay with relatives or strangers in urban areas where they are to be given food, shelter, and a chance to go to school, in exchange for performing chores around the house. Instead, often in their new homes they become domestic slaves, performing menial tasks for no pay. Like Jenika, they may be mistreated and neglected, and the promise of attending school may never come true.

These children are constantly reminded that they do not belong, that they are not wanted, that they are objects to be used and discarded. They are made to feel like their voices, their lives, will never count.

But the authors of this book are working to change that.

Who are the Restavek Freedom Writers?

The courageous young women who wrote this book—Kathia, Lisna, Marilene, Victoria, Rose, and Yolencia—are members of a transitional home in Port-au-Prince sponsored by the Restavek Freedom Foundation, a nonprofit organization whose mission is to end child slavery in Haiti.

These authors understand the struggle of girls like Jenika, and they used their own heartache as well as their own determination to write this original story. They knew that their voices could be the most powerful forces in making a change.

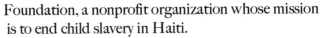

How Did They Do It?

Every day for a week during the summer of 2014, these young women gathered together to write. They broke into two teams and worked in collaboration with staff from Shout Mouse Press as well as dedicated Haitian college students who were passionate about the cause. They brainstormed original characters and plotlines inspired by the real-life struggles of *restavek* children, and then drafted, developed, and revised their stories.

The result is the book you hold in your hand: a heartfelt and original story designed to **start a revolution** and **stop the practice of *restavek*.**

Why Write Books?

There are many reasons that the *restavek* practice persists in Haiti – ranging from economic hardship to cultural attitudes towards children – but one of the major barriers is awareness.

Many people outside of Haiti don't know that this injustice is happening, and people within Haiti are just beginning to talk about it. That's why the Restavek Freedom Writers set out to become authors. Their mission is to awaken their reading public by:

> instilling **empathy** for children living in *restavek*
> creating **outrage** at the injustice of exploitation and abuse
> providing **inspiration** to stand up, speak up, and make a change

By writing these books, these authors take control of their stories, reshaping them with power and possibility and hope.

By reading these books, you are letting the thousands of children living in *restavek* know that their story matters, and that their voices are being heard.

> "The word *restavek* is often avoided in Haiti, out of shame that some people still participate in the gruesome act of enslaving someone else. Although it is common in the capital of Haiti, many young adults who I've talked to had never heard of the word *restavek*. This is what I believe makes this practice so dangerous, and yet so permissible, because many people don't know it still exists, or simply choose to ignore it."
>
> **- Laeticia**
> *Haitian college student / story intern*

What Can You Do?

Help us spread the word. These books need to reach as many readers as possible in order to make these voices heard. Share the books with your friends and family, schools and faith communities, book clubs and neighborhood groups. Or commit to purchase books for distribution within Haiti or your own community. Books can be purchased at:

> restavekfreedom.org
>
> shoutmousepress.org/restavek-freedom

For purchases of 100+ books, contact info@shoutmousepress.org. *Proceeds from book sales support girls removed from the restavek system and help champion other unheard voices.*

Arrange a book event. Bring people together to discuss the issue of *restavek* within your neighborhood, school, faith community, or book club. Authors and/or facilitators may be available upon request. Contact info@restavekfreedom.org for more information.

Stand up for children. If you know of a child being trafficked or exploited, do something about it. Be an advocate for those who need it most.

> "From the time I was a young girl, my mother always taught me to open my eyes to the injustice in my country. The *restavek* system is one of the most horrible issues, and it needs immediate recognition and action. Hopefully through these books we will be able to open the eyes of people all over the world to the issue of child slavery in Haiti in order to come together and put it to an end."
>
> - Colleen
> *Haitian college student / story intern*

In Haiti: Call the 188 Haiti-wide HELP line

In the United States:
National Human Trafficking Resource Center
traffickingresourcecenter.org
1.888.373.7888 or text HELP to BeFree (233733)

Get involved. If you are moved by this story and want to do more, learn about supporting the work of Restavek Freedom Foundation. Sponsor a child, host an exhibit, fundraise, or donate.

You can help bring an end to child slavery in Haiti.

Meet the Authors

Kathia, *17 years old*

When I have free time I like to play guitar, and I love reading, drawing, and painting. I'm really cool and relaxed. When I get older I would like to be a psychologist because I want to help others who've been traumatized.

"I've done some writing before. I wrote a story about how you should never listen to the bad things people are saying about you. I really appreciate the work we did because many people do not know the story of these children living in misery."

Victoria, *17 years old*

I love music, playing guitar, and writing poetry. The poems are for my country, HAITI. I would like to be a music star, and an accountant, and a scientist. I would like to write songs about the situation of children in Haiti to bring about a change.

"I love that every day we got together and put our heads together to create the stories. I would like people to know that the lives these children are living are not normal. Kids should be able to be whatever they want to be in life."

Marilene, *14 years old*

I am funny, and I think that a lot of people think so, too. They think that I am a good person and that I have talent. My talent is singing and drawing. To have fun, I like watching TV.

"When writing this book, the ideas come quick, and I have a lot to say, but I am very shy."

Rose, *16 years old*

I am a happy person. I love making friends with people who know what real friendship is. I love doing hair and nails.

"It's important for the *restavek* system to end because it's immoral. People should talk about this system in church to help end it. We must show how important children are to the country's future."

Lisna, *18 years old*

I love going to school because I want to be something in life so I can help my little sisters. I would like to become a psychologist. I like to comfort others. I like to give people advice that can help them.

"I would like people to know that there are many people who take other people's children and say they treat them well, but they actually treat them badly. To me, children who are suffering, they should be given what they need."

Yolencia, *12 years old*

I like to read, eat, sleep, and play in my free time. I also have been crocheting since the age of 7. I like to joke around, but I am also shy, and I am a good friend. I think that other people think I'm nice.

"When people don't take this seriously, it hurts me. That's why I love this project. I want those reading this book to see the misery of *restavek* children and to help these children not go through all this misery. I want the system to end."

Acknowledgments

The Restavek Freedom Writer books could not have been possible without the dedication and support of a number of hard-working folks who believed in the importance of empowering these young women to write and share their stories. In particular, we thank:

Laeticia Hollant, Sarah Nerette, Cortney Zamor, and Colleen Zamor, all Haitian natives and current U.S. college students, for being the dedicated story scribes who helped these authors capture their voices on the page. These young women led writing sessions, translated for Shout Mouse staff, and created welcoming, joyful environments for the authors. We simply could not have done this without these committed young women. We thank fellow college student Arielle Accede as well for her time, and Steven Baboun of *Humans of Haiti* for his tremendous photographs of the writing process!

Michelle Marrion, for being essential to the project on multiple fronts: as a talented and compassionate videographer and photographer, and also as a translator, both in-person and in writing. We are grateful to Michelle for translating both books, and to Christina Guérin for her expertise in copy-editing in Creole.

Emily Iddings, for her beautiful, powerful illustrations. Emily used her love of Haiti and her passion for ending the system of *restavek* to bring these books to life, and we are grateful!

We also thank Sarah Cooke, Christine Lee Buchholz, Adeline Bien-Aime, and Regine Benoit for their essential input on the books and support of our authors during the writing process. The production of these books would also not be possible without the generous financial support of Stan and Marilyn Forston, Tom and Amelia Crutcher, Mary Hardesty, Erin McDonough, and many others who contributed to the project.

And finally we want to thank the courageous authors of these books, who serve as beacons of hope, renewal, and freedom for people everywhere, and whose powerful stories will inspire the revolution of justice of which they dream.

Joan Conn,
Restavek Freedom Foundation
Executive Director

Kathy Crutcher,
Shout Mouse Press
Founder

About Restavek Freedom Foundation

Restavek Freedom Foundation is a nonprofit organization based in Port-au-Prince, Haiti and Cincinnati, Ohio with a mission to end child slavery in Haiti in our lifetime. Since our inception in 2007, Restavek Freedom has worked on behalf of the 300,000 children living as *restavek* in Haiti. We advocate for children by providing educational opportunities for those living in *restavek,* influence communities to help change cultural norms regarding *restavek,* and mobilize community leaders to stand up for freedom.

www.RestavekFreedom.org

About Shout Mouse Press

Shout Mouse Press is a writing program and publishing house for unheard voices. We were founded in Washington, DC in 2014. Shout Mouse partners with nonprofit organizations serving communities in need to design book projects that help further their missions. Our authors have produced original children's books, memoir collections, and novels-in-stories.

www.ShoutMousePress.org